# BE BRAVE, BABY RABBIT

CREATED BY LUCY BATE

## STORY BY FRAN MANUSHKIN
## PICTURES BY DIANE DE GROAT

Crown Publishers, Inc., New York

Text copyright © 1990 by Crown Publishers, Inc.
Illustrations copyright © 1990 Diane de Groat
All rights reserved. No part of this book may be reproduced or
transmitted in any form or by any means, electronic or
mechanical, including photocopying, recording, or by any
information storage and retrieval system, without permission in
writing from the publisher.
Published by Crown Publishers, Inc., a Random House company,
225 Park Avenue South, New York, New York 10003
CROWN is a trademark of Crown Publishers, Inc.
Manufactured in Hong Kong

Library of Congress Cataloging-in-Publication Data
Manushkin, Fran. Be brave, baby rabbit / created by Lucy Bate ;
written by Fran Manushkin ; illustrated by Diane de Groat.
p.   cm.
Summary: While playing follow-the-leader with his big sister,
Baby Rabbit can't manage to jump over a bushel basket; but, after
he stands up to a Halloween monster, he has the confidence
to make the leap.
ISBN 0-517-57573-6 (trade)—ISBN 0-517-57574-4 (lib. bdg.)
[1. Brothers and sisters—Fiction. 2. Rabbits—Fiction.] I. Bate, Lucy.
II. De Groat, Diane, ili. III. Title. PZ7.M3195Bae 1990
[E]—dc20   89-49460
CIP
AC

10 9 8 7 6 5 4 3 2 1   First Edition

For Daniel Jacobson
F.M.

One sunny Halloween the Rabbit
family was out in the garden.
Father and Mother Rabbit were
picking apples. Little Rabbit and
Baby Rabbit were playing follow
the leader.

Little Rabbit walked across
a log.

So did Baby Rabbit.

Little Rabbit tossed an acorn
up and caught it.

And so did Baby Rabbit.

Little Rabbit said, "I bet you can't do *this*!" She took a deep breath and a great big jump—over a basket of apples.

"Sure, I can do that!" bragged Baby Rabbit. He took a deep breath and a great big jump—and tumbled to the ground. "Ouch, ouch!" he yelled, and he started to cry.

Quickly, Mother
picked up Baby Rabbit
and hugged him close
to her. "Thank
goodness it's just a
scratch," said Mother.
"Come inside and I'll
make it better."

Very gently Mother washed the dirt off Baby Rabbit's nose and dabbed on medicine.

"I want a big bandage!" sniffled Baby Rabbit.

"Of course!" agreed Mother, and she put it on and gave him a little kiss.

Little Rabbit watched Mother kissing Baby Rabbit. "Oh, Mommy," Little Rabbit said. "Come and help me put on my costume. It's time to go trick-or-treating."

"I'm going too!" said Baby Rabbit.

"Do we have to take him?" asked Little Rabbit. "Isn't he too small?"

"I'm not too small," said Baby Rabbit.

"Of course you aren't," said Mother Rabbit. "We are all going together."

Baby Rabbit got into his lion costume. "Grrr!" he growled.

"Whoo-hoo-hoo!" Little Rabbit hooted. "I'm a brave Indian princess!"

As they all hurried out the door, Father came in carrying the basket of apples. "Have fun, everyone! By the time you are back, there'll be hot apple pie to eat."

Little Rabbit led the way to the first house. "I love Halloween! It's so spooky!" she said. Little Rabbit knocked on the door as hard as she could and shouted, "Trick or treat!"

"Mommy!" Baby Rabbit said when the door opened. "Mommy, it's a witch!"

"It's Mary Woodchuck," Mother Rabbit said, smiling. "She's wearing a costume, just like you."

"Oh!" Baby Rabbit peeked from behind his tail and put out his paw for a treat.

Then they walked to the house across the road. "Trick or treat!" called out Little Rabbit.

"Trick or treat!" echoed Baby Rabbit.

"Well, what have we here?" wondered Mrs. Squirrel. "I've never seen a lion with a bandage on."

"Baby Rabbit fell down!" Little Rabbit explained. "He fell right on his nose!"

"Ouch!" said Mrs. Squirrel. "I'll bet that hurt." She gave Baby Rabbit a pat on the head and a little bag of popcorn.

At the next house Baby Rabbit said, "I want to knock on the door this time!" And he did. He knocked as hard as he could and shouted, "Trick or treat!"

"Oh, my," said Mr. Raccoon, "what a fierce young lion." Baby Rabbit smiled proudly as Mr. Raccoon gave him a cookie. "Tell me," Mr. Raccoon said. "What happened to your nose?"

"I'll tell you what happened," said Little Rabbit.

"No!" said Baby Rabbit. "It's my nose! Don't tell!"

"You don't have to tell me," said Mr. Raccoon. "Let me see if I can guess. Were you riding on a bucking bronco, and he tossed you off his back?"

"No, no, no!" said Baby Rabbit with a little smile.

"Let me guess again," said Mr. Raccoon. "Were you rescuing Little Rabbit from a sneaky crocodile?"

"I would if I saw one!" Baby Rabbit shouted. And he leaped away with a growl.

Baby Rabbit growled all the way down the path. Suddenly he and Little Rabbit saw a huge purple monster running toward them, roaring!

"*Yeeeeek!*" Little Rabbit yelped, and hid behind a tree.

But Baby Rabbit didn't run. He glared at the monster and roared right back!

The scary monster stopped his roaring. He smiled and gave Baby Rabbit a hug. It was Grandpa Rabbit!

Baby Rabbit hugged his grandpa right back.

"My," said Little Rabbit, "You are really brave!"

"I am!" said Baby Rabbit. "I really am!"

Baby Rabbit couldn't wait to get home and tell Father Rabbit what had happened. "Daddy!" he shouted. "Trick-or-treating was scary, and it was lots of fun!"

Father nodded. "Lots of things are scary and fun!"

"I scared a monster," said Baby Rabbit proudly. "I roared and jumped all around!"

"Good for you!" Father smiled.

"Daddy, do you know what?" said Baby Rabbit. "Maybe I can jump over those apples, too!"

"I bet you can!" agreed Father.

Little Rabbit said, "On your mark, get set, go!" Baby Rabbit took a big deep breath—and jumped right over those apples!

"Hurray! You did it!" Mother and Father cheered.

"I did it!" shouted Baby Rabbit.

"Now," said Father, "how about some pie?"

"Grrr!" roared Baby Rabbit. "I'm as hungry as a lion. I'd like the biggest slice!"

And that's just what he ate.